## Poems for the Young at Heart

This is the third poetry collection by former teacher, **Tim Hopkins**, the first having been entitled, *Epitaph for an Auctioneer & Other Poems*, and the second, *Wittgenstein's Football Tactics & Other Poems.* In addition to poetry for adults and children, Tim Hopkins has published two novels for teenagers, and written humorous material for comedians and cartoonists. He has also composed songs that have been performed and recorded in the UK and the USA.

By the same Author -

# Poems for the Young at Heart

## Tim Hopkins

**Arena Books**

First published in 2021 by Arena Books

Arena Books
6 Southgate Green
Bury St. Edmunds
IP33 2BL


www.arenabooks.co.uk

*Distributed in America by Ingram International, One Ingram*
*Blvd., P.O. Box 3006, La Vergne, TN 37086-1985, USA.*

Tim Hopkins
*Poems for the Young at Heart*

British Library cataloguing in Publication Data. A Catalogue
record for this book is available from the British Library.

ISBN-13   978-1-911593-91-1
BIC classifications:-  DCF.

Cover design
by Anna Gatt

Typeset in
Times New Roman

# CONTENTS

## Children & Teachers

## Football

## All the Fun of the Fair

## Light-Hearted

# CHILDREN AND TEACHERS

## 1
## Leading In

"Mustn't run, Year One!
What a crew, Year Two!
Mind my tea, Year Three!
Watch that door, Year Four!
Look alive, Year Five!
Cut those tricks, Year Six!"

## 2
## Peter

Why is Peter always late?
Can't his feet increase their rate?
Would it help to roller skate?
Could he be dispatched as freight?
Is it learnt or just innate
Being last one through the gate?
Why this mean and selfish trait?
Why is Peter always late?

3
## Calling the Register

Eileen Back
Robin Banks
Edna Book
Flora Boxer
Henrietta Bunn
Iona Castle
Neil Downe
Laurie Driver
Daisy Fields
Ada Friend
Crispin Hand
Isobel Hurd
Esau Katz
Nita Ladd
Mona Lott
Rhoda Lyon
Ewan Mee
Owen Money
Ida Payne
Poppy Sellers
Bertha Shipp
Netta Trout
Anton Twigg
Dale Walker

## 4
## Mr Flack

Our class has got a student
His name is Mr Flack,
He wears a silver earring
His hair is down his back.

He's very kind and friendly
We know his name is Dave,
But sometimes it's too noisy
And children won't behave.

He wears a *Greenpeace* t-shirt
A cap and faded jeans,
He says he is a vegan
And lives on runner beans.

He plays guitar in lessons
He lets the class join in,
We clap and stamp in rhythm
And make an awful din.

Miss Grant's a better teacher
She's strict and keeps her cool,
But Mr Flack is funny
And brightens up the school.

5
## Mrs Smythe

If we're bad Miss Robbins shouts,
Miss Wilshaw cancels games,
Miss Henderson will keep us in,
Miss Withers calls us names,
But Mrs Smythe won't punish us
She'll fix us with a gaze
Until the class is silent
And no one disobeys.

6
## The Joker

Our teacher tries to tell us jokes
But always get them wrong,
He's like a nervous singer
Who doesn't know the song;
He'll get it right till halfway through
Then lose the story's thread –
Or if he gets the telling right
The punchline's lost instead.
"I'm sorry, boys and girls," he says,
"My mind's a blank, I fear,"
Then laughs when he remembers it –
The joke we never hear.

## 7
## A Humourless Teacher

A humourless teacher called Hills
Cured insomnia without using pills,
His words dull and boring
Led quickly to snoring
For such were his medical skills.

## 8
## School Medicals

You have to take your shirt off
For Dr Smedley-Gumm,
He taps you with his fingers
And pokes you with his thumb.

He shines things in your eyeballs,
Your nose, your mouth and ears,
And listens to your chest and tum
But won't say what he hears.

9
## The PE Lesson

Why are girls better at skipping
And keeping their balance on beams?
And why are they better at cartwheels
And quicker at getting in teams?

Why are boys better at climbing
And throwing and kicking a ball?
And why are they always such show-offs
And noisier leaving the hall?

## 10
## Wrigglers

Wrigglers don't like PE,
Teachers know their names,
They make up weak excuses
To wriggle out of games.

Frankie has no plimsolls,
Tracey's lost her kit,
Wrigglers tell such whopping lies
And never mind a bit.

Beth has a headache,
Pete a painful arm,
Wrigglers tell their awful fibs
Then add a touch of charm.

Shaun has got the toothache,
Jen a touch of 'flu,
Wrigglers' noses grow so long
They reach to Timbuktu.

Bill has got a stomach pain,
Charlotte has a cold,
Wrigglers' tales are sometimes new
But mostly very old.

Wrigglers don't like PE,
Teachers know their names,
They make up weak excuses
To wriggle out of games.

## 11
## Questions

Maria answer well in class
The teacher knows she's bright,
And when Maria's hand goes up
She gets the answer right.

Amanda keeps her head well down
The teacher knows she's slow,
And if a question comes her way
She often doesn't know.

Amanda's kind and cheerful
A friend who really cares,
But no one likes Maria
Who's mean and never shares.

## 12
## Tracy

Why is Tracy top in tests? –
She's not the swotty sort,
Her dad says school is stupid,
Her brother's been in court.

She wears her sister's cast-offs,
Her home's a tiny flat,
But Tracy's good at netball
And loves to joke and chat.

She's popular and pretty,
The nicest girl I know,
She's sweet and kind and clever
And never tells you so.

13
## Gossip

Sarah says Jill is a show-off,
Amanda says Jean took her sweet,
Lucinda says Lucy's a bully
And Ella says Bella's a cheat;
Peter says Mark's got diseases,
Priscilla says Paul is too posh,
Belinda says Laura's a liar
And Michael says John doesn't wash.

Gossip is usually nasty –
Why don't we say something that's nice? –
Like "Melanie leant me her pencil"
Or "Joseph knows lots about mice"
Or "Sophie's an excellent singer"
"Samantha is kind to her cat" –
If only we'd look on the bright side
Our school would be better for that.

## 14
### Reggie Rix

Reggie Rix wears dirty shirts
He doesn't wash his face,
His coat would make a scarecrow blush
His hair is out of place.

Reggie Rix wears ragged jeans
His shoes have come apart,
But just below his grimy skin
There beats a loving heart.

15
## An Upset

When Paul McKevitt's mother died
He took the week off school,
He came back on the Tuesday
And hadn't got a note,
Miss Robson said she didn't mind
And cried at what he wrote.

## 16
## Jasper Dwight

Jasper Dwight wears fancy clothes
(Dad's got pots of money),
Spends his break-time cracking jokes –
No one thinks they're funny.

Jasper Dwight is brought to school
In a brand new Roller,
Mother wears the best fur coats,
Dad, a suit and bowler.

Jasper Dwight learns martial arts
When he's mad he'll thump you,
One day swears he'll be your friend
Next day wants to dump you.

Jasper Dwight's a horsey boy
Rides a jumping pony,
Wins rosettes but riders say
Jasper's mean and moany.

Jasper Dwight sits next to me
He thinks he's super-cool,
But I think Jasper's stuck-up
A show-off and a fool.

## 17
## The Scatterbrain

"Lost your pencil?  Lost your book?
Lost your dinner money?
One day you'll lose your head my lad
And that will *not* be funny."

Ronnie didn't hear a word
The angry teacher said,
His ears weren't in the classroom
But where he'd left his head.

## 18
### The Mathematician

A schoolboy of minimal sense
Had a mind both befuddled and dense,
When asked three add three
He replied, "Let me see,
I think that makes fifty-eight pence."

19
## The Clear-Out

Today I cleared my desk out
And stuffed the junk in bags,
Amazing what I found
From pies to football mags;
Dried-out blobs of toffee,
A mouldy apple core,
A Christmas card from Pete,
The missing woodwork saw;
Crumbs from ginger biscuits,
An absence note I wrote,
Buckled cans of cola,
Amanda Vincent's coat;
Photos of my cousin,
Postcards from my aunt,
Party invitations,
A withered spider plant;
Paper clips and biros,
A pencil (badly chewed),
A shoelace and a sock,
A picture (somewhat rude);
Today I cleared my desk out,
It's neat as neat can be,
But will it stay this way? –
We'll have to wait and see!

## 20
## The Proud Parent

When Jimmy Thompson's mother
Came storming into school,
She said, "My boy's a good boy
Who never plays the fool,
So why," she asked the teacher,
"Send Jimmy to the Head?
If other boys are naughty
Why blame my Jim instead?"
"You've got it wrong," said Teacher,
"Your Jimmy's not a saint –
At home he may be quiet
But here he's not so quaint;
He throws his books and pencils,
He trips up older girls,
This morning in assembly
He pigged on walnut whorls;
He cheeks the dinner ladies
He lets down teachers' tyres,
He threatens younger children
And tries to start small fires."
"But otherwise," said Mother,
"He's wonderful, I'm sure,
A perfect little poppet
A boy you must adore."

## 21
## Prayer at Home Time

*"Hands together, close your eyes,"*
(Day is over – how time flies.)
*"God protect us through the night,"*
(Glad I got my spellings right.)
*"God defend us from our fears,"*
(Got a star for art – three cheers!)
*"God be there when morning comes,"*
(Wish I understood those sums.)
*"Be with us our whole life through,"*
(Wrote a six-page story – phew!)
*"Guard us till we meet again,"*
(Here's our bit at last – )
*"AMEN!"*

# FOOTBALL

## 22
## A Football Alphabet

A    attacked it
B    bent it
C    controlled it
D    dribbled it
E    elbowed it
F    flicked it
G    gathered it
H    headed it
I    intercepted it
J    juggled it
K    kicked it
L    lobbed it
M    missed it
N    nudged it
O    offloaded it
P    passed it
Q    quitted it
R    rifled it
S    skyed it
T    trapped it
U    unleashed it
V    volleyed it
W    won it
X    xtra-timed it
Y    yielded it
Z    zapped it

23
## The Art of Football

Liverpool and Everton drew,
Arsenal and Tottenham coloured in.

24
**Football Skills**

Trap it
Tap it

Back it
Whack it

Clear it
Steer it

Belt it
Welt it

Chip it
Clip it

Kick it
Flick it

Win it
Spin it

Block it
Knock it

Slow it
Toe it

Stun it
Run it

Swerve it
Curve it

## 25
## Goalkeeper

Standing tall between the posts
He's agile, brave, strong and brave
Now dives at forwards' flailing feet
Now makes a stunning save.

At goal-kicks strikes the ball so hard
He flights it up and away,
And thereby starts a fresh attack
Brings forwards into play.

At penalties he tries to judge
Which way the ball will go,
The options: centre, left or right –
And will it be high or low?

Though injuries may happen
He accepts his hazardous role,
For courage is the watchword
Of the man who plays in goal.

## 26
## Defender

Six foot two and twelve stone five
The big man at the back,
Positioning and timing
Make up for speed I lack.

My strongest point is heading
Here height comes into play,
I rise above the strikers
And head the ball away.

Of yellow cards and penalties
I'm constantly aware,
So when I'm breaking up attacks
My tackling's hard, but fair.

## 27
## Midfielder

I'm not the tallest player
And I'm somewhat slight of frame,
But skill and speed of thought I bring
To each and every game.

Sometimes I'm playing way up front
Sometimes I'm tracking back
And in my holding role I turn
Defence into attack.

Sometimes I score a long-range goal
Last year I netted nine,
Or make a last-ditch clearance
When our keeper's off his line.

Passing is my strong point
But I have to tackle, too,
So good technique and fitness
Define me through and through.

## 28
## Striker

My job is simple – scoring goals –
And I'm proud to tell my story,
For when my efforts bulge the net
I'm the one who gets the glory.

Free kicks and corners I enjoy
Though defenders may be tall,
Spring-heeled I rise the highest
And goalward head the ball.

Some people say I'm arrogant
Big-headed and conceited,
They may be right, but thanks to me
This year we're undefeated.

## 29
### A Testing Time

After school we had a trial
For the Year Six football team,
I did the very best I could
To achieve my sporting dream.

Next day I looked at the notice-board
The Team was as expected,
I felt both sad and angry –
I hadn't been selected.

30
## Dennis Jones

Dennis Jones is shy in class,
He's not much good at sums,
When adding up he has to use
His fingers and his thumbs.

Dennis Jones is weak with words
He gets his spellings wrong,
And when he writes a story
It's only six lines long.

Dennis Jones is never slow
When playing for the team,
At football he's a natural
And plays it like a dream.

## 31
## The Football Captain

We'll play *St Martha's* after school
But not if there's more rain,
I watch the sky in geography
In maths I watch again.

The autumn clouds are streaky grey
Like white paint stirred with black,
Although I've lots of work to do
My eyes keep going back.

But this could be my lucky day
The sun comes shining through,
The breeze picks up and clears the clouds
To show a sky of blue.

We have a test before the bell
I get the lowest score,
My heart is thumping in my chest
The match is on for sure.

## 32
## The Team Sheet

At half-past two on Thursday
The football team went up –
St John's against St Wilfred's
The final of the cup.

I'd played so badly last time
I thought I'd lose my place,
My heart was beating wildly
The fear showed in my face.

I scanned the list so quickly
I couldn't find my name,
Then someone said, "You're in then?" –
My pride was tinged with shame.

## 33
## Our Teacher

Miss Wilkins is a footballer
She plays in a women's side,
A fast and skilful forward
She plays on the right out wide.

She's passed her referee's exam
She's fit and knows the rules,
And referees our matches
When we're playing other schools.

**ALL THE FUN OF THE FAIR**

34
**The Fair Comes to Town**

Trucks with equipment arrive in a fleet,
Cars towing caravans block the main street,
Everyone's cheerful and no one feels down,
This is the day when the fair comes to town.

Men are unloading the rides and the tents,
Ponies are grazing while tied to a fence,
Everyone's cheerful and no one feels down,
This is the day when the fair comes to town.

Children are playing, their dogs running free,
Cooking smells good, it's a fry-up for tea,
Everyone's cheerful and no one feels down,
This is the day when the fair comes to town.

## 35
## Fairground Lights

Crimson, claret, scarlet, red,
Paintbox patterns tree-top high,
Every shade of every colour
Summer night-time fairground sky.

Saffron, yellow, lemon, gold,
Pastel tints of butterfly,
Every shade of every colour,
Summer night-time fairground sky.

Lilac, turquoise, purple, blue,
Liquid tones of dragonfly,
Every shade of every colour,
Summer night-time fairground sky.

## 36
## Helter-Skelter

Helter-skelter
Straw mat riding,
Downward sliding,
Swiftly gliding.

Helter-skelter,
No hands gripping,
Earthward slipping,
Plunging, dipping.

Helter-skelter,
Spiral racing,
High-speed chasing,
Friends outpacing.

Helter-skelter,
Final-bending,
Bumpy ending
Hands extending.

37
**Swingboat**

Swingboat, swingboat,
Swing me up high,
Swing me gently
Into the sky.

Swingboat, swingboat,
Swing to and fro,
Blue sky over,
Green field below.

Swingboat, swingboat,
Sail through the air,
Backwards, forwards,
Wind in my hair.

Swingboat, swingboat,
Swing me to sleep,
Swing me softly
Counting my sheep.

## 38
## Ghost Train

Ghouls are shrieking,
Hinges creaking,
Goblins squeaking,
On the ghost train.

Spooks are prowling,
Phantoms scowling,
Furies howling,
On the ghost train.

Cobwebs lashing,
Lightning flashing,
Thunder crashing,
On the ghost train.

Fiends' eyes gleaming,
Ogres scheming,
Banshees screaming,
On the ghost train.

## 39
## The Big Wheel

The big wheel stops, you climb aboard,
And sail towards the sun,
You don't like heights but being scared
Is really half the fun.

The big wheel gives a bird's eye view
Of people in the town,
Who look like toyland figures
Because they're so far down.

40
## Hampstead Fair

Mum took me to the fair one night,
"Stay close to me," she said, "stick tight."
But I walked off without a care
And soon was lost at Hampstead Fair.

I looked for Mum and called her name,
But no one answered, no one came;
I searched in panic everywhere
For I was lost at Hampstead Fair.

With happy faces streaming past
My courage failed and tears fell fast,
Their happiness I couldn't share
For I was lost at Hampstead Fair.

Then suddenly Mum caught my arm,
"You stupid child, you'll come to harm!"
I didn't speak – I didn't dare –
For I'd been lost at Hampstead Fair.

41
## Madame Zelda

Madame Zelda tells your fortune
In a tiny fairground tent,
Her predictions are amazing
And you'll think five pounds well-spent.

Madame Zelda will reveal to you
Events both great and small,
For she can see the future
In her magic crystal ball.

42
**Balloon**

I buy a balloon as I'm leaving the fair,
It's filled with a gas which is lighter than air,
I'm hoping the person who finds my balloon
Will see my address on the tag and write soon.

I watch my balloon as it sails through the air,
It's travelling fast, but I've no idea where,
It may stay in England or reach other lands,
I'm hoping for France, but it's out of my hands.

43
## The Fair Outside My Window

On my ceiling shadows creeping,
Ten o'clock I should be sleeping.

Silhouettes on curtains flicker,
Rides start slowly, then go quicker.

Organs playing, drumbeat drumming,
In my head a rhythm thrumming.

Footsteps in the roadway clatter,
Young men shout and women chatter.

Fast food vans sell burgers, curries,
Queues are long, but no one hurries.

On my ceiling shadows creeping,
Ten o'clock I should be sleeping.

## 44
## The One Who Missed the Fair

The nurse has said goodnight
But I can't get to sleep,
I lift the curtain up
Across the fields I peep;
The fairground lights still shine
I wish I could be there,
Instead of ill in bed
The one who missed the fair.

The nurse says I'll get well
This is no time for tears,
But when I close my eyes
There's music in my ears;
The fairground organ plays
I wish I could be there,
Instead of ill in bed
The one who missed the fair.

## 45
## Fairground Sunday Morning

Empty dodgems in the rain
Sideshows under awning,
Big wheel swaying in the wind
Fairground Sunday morning.

Ponies huddle close for warmth
Guard dog barks a warning,
Cats sleep under caravans
Fairground Sunday morning.

46
## The Fair is Leaving Town

Ringing hammers echo
The rides are taken down,
Trailers quickly loaded
The fair is leaving town.

Caravans are moving
Through green fields turned to brown,
Stray dogs running with them
The fair is leaving town.

47
## The Driver

I drive a fairground lorry
On the lonely roads at night,
With the last town half-forgotten
And the next one out of sight.

# LIGHT-HEARTED

## 48
### You Are What You Eat

A health-conscious mother from Kew
Put a handful of nails in the stew,
She said to son Brian
"Your body needs iron
And a top-up is long overdue."

## 49
## Mimi

Overeating was Mimi's disgrace,
She'd an appetite vulgar and base,
And the food that she gobbled
Soon afterwards wobbled
At the opposite end from her face.

51
**Foodie**

A greedy young fellow from Hurst
With incredible hunger was cursed
His tum grew so vast
All the town heard the blast
When like a balloon he just burst.

51
## Weight-Watcher

Tubby Sam Warner
Sat in a sauna
Sweating off burgers and pie,
He pulled in his tum
Which reduced his girth some
And said, "What a slim boy am I!"

## 52
## Emotional

A sensitive schoolgirl from Crewe
When she met you would cry out, "Yoo-hoo!"
If you didn't reply
She would sobbingly cry:
"I'm so sad – you don't love me – boo-hoo!"

## 53
## Missing

Little Bo Peep has lost her beep
And doesn't know where to find it,
Her mobile phone
Is out on loan
With a friend she asked to mind it.

## 54
## Secret Message

I'm fonder view,
A door ewe,
Were ship ewe,
Add mire ewe,
My art beat sly Kenny thing.

## 55
## Home Truths

You are...

Infan-TILE
Un-HINGE-d,
Inde-FENCE-ible,
Con-FUSE-d,
PHONE-y...

SWITCH-ed on,
FIRE-d up,
Diplom-ATTIC,
De-LIGHT-ful,
A-DOOR-able.

## 56
## Happy

Giggle at a squiggle,
Laugh at a scarf,
Chuckle at a buckle,
Smile at a stile,
Guffaw at a claw,
Titter at a knitter,
Chortle at a portal,
Grin at a pin.

## 57
## Superstition

Avoid the pavement mortar
Step only on the squares
For ill-luck stalks the careless
Their future life impairs.

No walking under ladders
This error prompts a curse
A fearsome doom awaits you
Believe this warning verse.

The number thirteen should be shunned
Its influence is malign
Instead heed three and seven
When life should turn out fine.

But if your mind is logical
These jinxes have no power
Bad luck is not foreshadowed
No need to meekly cower.

## 58
### Sneezes

"ATISHOO!  ATISHOO!
I wish you'd not issue
That spray of germ-carrying rheum."

"A tissue, a tissue,
This hankie I issue
And beg you stop rheuming my room!"

59
## Doctor! Doctor!

She said to her doctor:
"My feet really pong,
And the scent of my body's unusually strong."
The doctor consulted a book which he showed her:
"Here's what you need – BICARBONATE OF ODOUR."

She said to her doctor:
"My memory's gone –
I'd forget my own head if it wasn't screwed on."
The doctor was sure he could make her life easier:
"Here's what you need – MILK OF AMNESIA."

She said to her doctor:
"I eat too much pie,
Then I snort and I grunt and roll round in a sty."
The doctor winked twice, gave her tummy three digs:
"Here's what you need – SYRUP OF PIGS."

## 60
## What If

What if the leg could bite the dog
Or the tree could fell the axe?
What if the lip could sting the wasp
Or the hammer was hit by the tacks?

What if the sky fell out of the rain
Or the earth shone up at the sun?
What if the beach splashed over the waves
Or the bullet fired the gun?

What if the picture painted the brush
Or the music played the bands?
What if the hair cut the scissors
Or the soap was washed by the hands?

What if the cake could chew the teeth
Or the foot was worn by the sock?
What if the goal scored the player
Or the tick made the sound of a tock?

What if the night was really the day
Or the sun was really the moon?
Then upside down would be downside up
And we'd celebrate Christmas in June.

## 61
## What am I?

I have keys that open no doors,
I have hammers that hit no nails,
I have strings that tie no knots,
I have notes that nobody reads.

I have no friends but can be harmonious,
I have no feelings but inspire emotion,
I have no morals but may be upright,
I have no ego but may be grand.

(answer: I am a piano)

## 62
## Facing the Music

Raymond and I stole some cash,
The local police made a dash,
And took to the station all three –
Dough...   Ray...   me...

## 63
## Vampires

The Vampires that Bite Necks in Gangs
Like a blood which is tasty and tangs,
When they've guzzled enough
Of the hot pulsing stuff
They say to their teeth: "Thank you fangs!"

## 64
## Night-Time Imaginings

Is the knocking in the pipe
A phantom with a drum?
Is the shadow on the wall
The ghost of Tweedledum?
Are silhouettes on curtains
Two headless spooks in coats?
Is the water in the gutters
Strong rum in giants' throats?
Is the squeaking garden gate
A fury screeching names?
Is the lightning in the wood
A dragon spitting flames?

65
## Night Secrets

As soon as you're sleeping
The bedroom wakes up,
Sidelight winks at lampshade,
Saucer chats to cup,
Curtains wave at windows,
Slippers dance on mats,
Cobwebs tickle corners,
Mittens juggle hats,
Wardrobe doors fly open,
Jumpers wrestle shirts
Jackets flap like eagles,
Trousers dance with skirts.

# CREATURES

## 66
## Camel

Shape lumpy,
Back humpy.
Legs clumpy,
Feet stumpy,
Ride bumpy,
Mood grumpy.

67
## King of the River

Do be wary of the hippo
For a boat he'll sometimes tippo
And the occupants unshippo
For an unexpected dippo.

68
## Snake

Be wary of the boa
When the sun is moving loa
And the village lanterns gloa
long the waterline.

Be wary of the boa
When the turning tide moves sloa
And your fishing boat you roa
long the waterline.

Be wary of the boa
From its top branch sliding loa
With its length uncoiling sloa
long the waterline.

## 69
## Whale

Who can fail
To admire the whale
The colossal scale
The flail of a tail
In calm or gale?
Let this splendour prevail
Let none curtail
The life of the whale.

70
## Life in the Ark

Lions roared,
Bulls gored,
Wasps stung,
Limpets clung,
Hyenas shrieked,
Skunks reeked,
Frogs leapt,
Cats crept,
Snakes coiled,
Oxen toiled,
Fleas jumped,
Sloths slumped,
Horses neighed,
Donkeys brayed,
Monkeys teased,
Bears squeezed,
Pigs squealed,
Pythons peeled,
Pumas pounced,
Kangaroos bounced,
Vultures flapped,
Crocodiles snapped,
Dogs growled,
Wolves howled,
Cocks crowed,
Fireflies glowed,
Woodpeckers drummed,
Bees hummed,
Tigers clawed,
Beavers gnawed.

## 71
## Animal Facts

Porcupines have fork-you spines,
The rattlesnake makes cattle quake,
The polar bear is shoal-aware,
Crocodiles have mocker smiles.

## 72
## Rod and Line

When fishing in a local stream
I caught a silver fish,
But from the hook
It gave a look
As if to make a wish;
That wish for me was plain to see:
"Don't pull me from my watery land
And clutch me in your warm, dry hand,
Just leave me swimming lazily,
Don't make me wriggle crazily –
Oh yes, oh yes, this is my wish.
Young lad, don't fish, don't fish, don't fish..."

## 73
## Music

I caught a springtime songbird
And kept him in a hut,
But there he never sang a note
His beak stayed firmly shut.

I talked to him so gently
I praised his woodland voice
But all I got was silence
Which left me with no choice...

I left the hut door open
He flew to the nearest tree
And there he sang his heart out
Happy to be free.

## 74
## Husky

Commands obeying,
Arctic sleighing,
Team-playing,
Strength displaying,
Goods conveying,
Task-staying,
Trust repaying,
Moon baying.

## Our Dogs

Poodles
Have oodles
Of charm
To disarm.

While brave GSDs
Will track and seize
The fugitive crook
And bring him to book.

The Labrador's fun
Is to work with the gun
Retrieving game
His claim to fame.

While the sporty Jack Russell
Without any fuss'll
Dispatch the rats
And shame the cats.

The rottweiler's muscle
Equips him to tussle
Aloof and hard –
The ideal guard.

While the border collie
Can herd without folly
No brain works faster
Than his, for his master.

And what an achiever!
The golden retriever
Such coolness of mind
When guiding the blind.

## 76
## Be Kind to Animals

Hug
A slug.

Chat
To rat.

Bow
To a cow.

Talk
To a hawk.

Dote
On a stoat.

Charm
a llama.

Be a honey
To a bunny.

--oOo--